7 ATE 9

THE UNTOLD STORY

Written by Tara Lazar

Illustrated by Ross MacDonald

Disney • HYPERION

LOS ANGELES   NEW YORK

To the students, faculty, and staff at Mount Prospect Elementary School
—TL

To all my grade school math teachers, who made numbers fun
—RM

Text copyright © 2017 by Tara Lazar
Illustrations copyright © 2017 by Ross MacDonald

First Edition, May 2017
3   5   7   9   10   8   6   4   2
FAC-029191-17227
Printed in Malaysia

This book is set in 20-point Columbus MT Pro/Monotype;
DHF Harry's Brush/Fontspring
Designed by Maria E Elias
The art in this book was created using colored pencils, watercolors,
and 19th-century wood type, then composed digitally using Photoshop.

Library of Congress Cataloging-in-Publication Data Control Number: 2016018849
ISBN 978-1-4847-1779-0

Reinforced binding

Visit www.DisneyBooks.com

I was dozing in my chair when an urgent banging on my office door bolted me awake.

It was **6**. Something had scared the pants off him.

"**7** is coming to get me," said **6**.

As a **Private I**, I'm used to his type—
numbers. They're always stuck in a problem.
But I knew about this **7** fella. He was odd.

"Take it easy, **6**," I said. "What's **7** up to?"

"Word on the street is that **7** ate **9**!
And now he's after me," said **6**.

"Well, technically, he's *always* after you,"
I said. "There's **5**, then **6**, then **7**."

"See, that proves it!"

I told **6** not to panic. "Stay here. I'll get to the root of this."

"I hope so!" said **6**. "I fear my days are numbered."

First I went looking for **8**. She's usually caught
between **7** and **9**.

I found her at the corner of Second Avenue and Fourth Street. But **8** knew nothing.

Nada.
    Zilch.

"If it's true," **8** said, "then I'm next in line!" In a flash, she took off her belt. Now **8** looked just like **0**.

Good disguise.

I needed a solid lead. I strolled into Café Uno, leaned on the counter, and ordered a slice of pi. **B**, the waitress, had the scoop.

"Yeah, I heard **7** ate **9**," she said.

"So you haven't seen **9** around?" I asked.

"Negative," said **B**. "He just disappeared."

So **9** was gone. I couldn't let **7** be the one who got away.

But I needed more data. I went to see **11**.
She and **7** are like two peas in a pod.

"**7** couldn't have done it," said **11**.
"He's on vacation."

"Are you sure?" I prodded.

"I'm positive! I saw him leave."

But if **7** was gone, then where was **9**?
It didn't add up.

Frustrated, I headed back uptown.
That's when I saw *him* crossing the street.
Finally, I put two and two together.

I had to get back to the office.
"On the double," I told the driver.

I busted through my office door and found **6** taking forty winks.

"I have solved this numerical nonsense," I cried. I grabbed **6** and turned him . . . upside down.

His true color was revealed.

Just as I suspected—my client,
6, was really **9**!

"You had everyone worried, **9**," I said.
"Why did you say that **7** ate **9**?"

"Because **7** gets all the attention!
'Lucky seven'!
'Seven Wonders of the World'!
'Snow White and the Seven Dwarfs'!"

Figures. **9** felt like he didn't measure up.

"*Seven,* *seven,* SEVEN! It's like I don't exist. Folks hurry right past me on their way to **10**. Don't even get me started on **10**. Everyone thinks he's perfect!"

I zeroed in on **9**. "Are you kidding?
You should be on cloud nine right now.
Happy as can be, the whole nine yards!"

"How come?" asked **9**.

"Because you've got NINE lives!"

That's when **11** showed up. "Look who's back!" she said.

It was **7**. "Umm," stammered **9**.
"No hard feelings, **7**, old pal?"

"Sure. Let's not be divided," **7** said.

7 seemed awfully pleased for a number who had been framed. "Why so happy, 7?" I asked.

"I just sailed the seven seas. I'm in seventh heaven!"

At last, everyone was back in order.
And now I could take letter cases again.
Letters can be wordy at times, but
they're A-OK in my book.

The next day, while dozing in my chair, my phone bolted me awake. I'd recognize her voice anywhere. It was 2 . . . with another problem to solve.

I've really got to change my number!